THE BOOK OF REPULSIVE WOMEN

Books by Djuna Barnes

The Book of Repulsive Women (1915; reprinted in 1989 and 1994)
A Book (1923)
Ladies Almanack (1928; reprinted in 1972 and 1992)
Ryder (1928; reprinted in 1979 and 1990)
A Night Among the Horses (1929)
Nightwood (1936; first American edition 1937; reprinted in
1949, 1950, 1961, 1963, 1966, and 1967)
The Antiphon (1958)
Selected Works (1962)
Spillway (1962; reprinted in 1972)
Smoke and Other Early Stories (1982; reprinted in 1987)
Interviews (1985)
New York (1989)

Djuna Barnes

The Book of

REPULSIVE
WOMEN

8 Rhythms and 5 Drawings

SUN &
MOON
CLASSICS
59

Los Angeles
SUN & MOON PRESS
1994

:ational Project, Inc.

6026 Wilshire Boulevard, Los Angeles, California 90036

This edition first published in paperback in 1994 by Sun & Moon Press
10 9 8 7 6 5 4 3 2 1
SECOND PAPERBACK EDITION
The Book of Repulsive Women was first published
as a Bruno Chap Book (Vol. II) in November 1915
First published in paperback by Sun & Moon Press in July 1989
as No. 1 of the *20 Pages* series.
Introduction ©1994 by Douglas Messerli
Biographical material ©1994 by Sun & Moon Press
All rights reserved

This book was made possible, in part, through an operational grant from
the Andrew W. Mellon Foundation, and through contributions to The
Contemporary Arts Educational Project, Inc.,
a nonprofit corporation

Cover: Djuna Barnes
Drawings: Djuna Barnes
Cover Design: Katie Messborn
Typography: Guy Bennett

LIBRARY OF CONGRESS CATALOGING IN PUBLICATION DATA
Barnes, Djuna [1892–1982]
The Book of Repulsive Women
p. cm – (Sun & Moon Classics: 59)
ISBN: 1-55713-192-9
I. Title. II. Series.
811'.54–dc20

Printed in the United States of America on acid-free paper.

Contents

A Note

First published in the Bruno Chap Books series in November, 1915, *The Book of Repulsive Women* remains today Djuna Barnes's least known and, in terms of its content, most accessible of her writings.

Certainly, it was not a book that Barnes herself highly valued, and one suspects that she would have characterized it, as she had all of her early journalism, as juvenilia. Whatever her view, she successfully suppressed a 1948 pirated edition, published as *Outcast Chapbook No. 14*. Bern Boyle Books published a small edition in 1989, and Sun & Moon published an edition, based on the original, in July of the same year.

The Bern Boyle version, however, brought up several interesting editorial questions, one of which, in particular, had troubled me since first encountering the Bruno Chap Book while compiling my 1976 bibliography of Djuna Barnes.

Barnes's writing is almost all inextricably connected with her art. The vast majority of the interviews, essays on theatre and other journalistic pieces, the novel *Ryder*, the collection of stories, *A Book*, and her *Ladies Almanack* were all published side by side with her art. Even *Nightwood* is heavily reliant on the 18th and 19th century tableaux vivants, which she describes as "living pictures." One might go far as to say that Barnes's literary method is, in fact, an "emblematic" one, in that her writing generally relies on visual elements that supplement, intensify, and clarify aspects of the language. What critics such as Joseph Frank have described as "momentary stops" in the narrative action are actually related to this emblematic method of writing, wherein Barnes visualizes (with art or words) the moral or psychological condition of her characters before representing them in action.

How peculiar, then, that her first book segregated drawings that were so clearly intended to relate directly to her poetry. As Bern Boyle so astutely recognized, certain of the drawings appear to fit on the page perfectly with the text. Having published our own edition exactly as it appeared in the original

Bruno Chap Book edition, I determined that when we reprinted we would reset these poems, pulling the art from the back of the book to the front, attempting to place the art in correspondence with the writing. My arrangement is not that of the Bern Boyle edition. Without knowing Barnes's original intentions, I felt editorially more comfortable placing the art on facing pages of the poems rather than on the same pages. Moreover, the art seemed to relate, in my mind, with poems different from those Bern Boyle had chosen. Others, doubtlessly, will disagree with my choices and, perhaps, with Bern Boyle's as well. Nonetheless, the art/poem relationship feels, in both editions, much closer to a book by Djuna Barnes than the original had.

Djuna Barnes, if she were not in fury, might well have laughed at the whole issue. Or, more likely, she would have demanded that we immediately destroy all copies. Ultimately, it is for her readers to decide the importance of this literary and artistic contribution. It is our goal, in our on-going publication of the writings of Barnes, simply to bring the material to the reader's attention.

–Douglas Messerli
Los Angeles

BRUNO CHAP BOOKS

DJUNA BARNES

THE BOOK OF REPULSIVE WOMEN

8 Rhythms and 5 Drawings

EDITED BY GUIDO BRUNO IN HIS GARRET ON
WASHINGTON SQUARE, NEW YORK

November, 1915   Fifteen Cents

SPECIAL SERIES

TO MOTHER
Who was more or less like All
mothers, but she was mine, and
so—She excelled.

From Fifth Avenue Up

SOMEDAY beneath some hard
      Capricious star–
Spreading its light a little
Over far,
We'll know you for the woman
That you are.

For though one took you, hurled you
Out of space,
With your legs half strangled
In your lace,
You'd lip the world to madness
On your face.

We'd see your body in the grass
With cool pale eyes.
We'd strain to touch those lang'rous
Length of thighs;
And hear your short sharp modern
Babylonic cries.

It wouldn't go. We'd feel you
Coil in fear
Leaning across the fertile
Fields to leer
As you urged some bitter secret
Through the ear.

We see your arms grow humid
In the heat;
We see your damp chemise lie
Pulsing in the beat
Of the over-hearts left oozing
At your feet.

See you sagging down with bulging
Hair to sip,
The dappled damp from some vague
Under lip.
Your soft saliva, loosed
With orgy, drip.

Once we'd not have called this
Woman you–
When leaning above your mother's
Spleen you drew
Your mouth across her breast as
Trick musicians do.

Plunging grandly out to fall
Upon your face.
Naked–female–baby
In grimace.
With your belly bulging stately
Into space.

In General

WHAT altar cloth, what rag of worth
Unpriced?
What turn of card, what trick of game
Undiced?
And you we valued still a little
More than Christ.

From Third Avenue On

AND now she walks on out turned feet
    Beside the litter in the street
Or rolls beneath a dirty sheet
       Within the town.
She does not stir to doff her dress,
She does not kneel low to confess,
A little conscience, no distress
       And settles down.

Ah God! she settles down we say;
It means her powers slip away
It means she draws back day by day
       From good or bad.

And so she looks upon the floor
Or listens at an open door
Or lies her down, upturned to snore
       Both loud and sad.

Or sits beside the chinaware,
Sits mouthing meekly in a chair,
With over–curled, hard waving hair
       Above her eyes.
Or grins too vacant into space–
A vacant space is in her face–
Where nothing came to take the place
       Of high hard cries.

Or yet we hear her on the stairs
With some few elements of prayers,
Until she breaks it off and swears
       A loved bad word.
Somewhere beneath her hurried curse,
A corpse lies bounding in a hearse;
And friends and relatives disperse,
       And are not stirred.

Those living dead up in their rooms
Must note how partial are the tombs,
That take men back into their wombs
       While theirs must fast.

And those who have their blooms in jars
No longer stare into the stars,
Instead, they watch the dinky cars–
       And live aghast.

Seen From The "L"

SO she stands–nude–stretching dully
    Two amber combs loll through her hair
A vague molested carpet pitches
Down the dusty length of stair.
She does not see, she does not care
    It's always there.

The frail mosaic on her window
Facing starkly toward the street
Is scribbled there by tipsy sparrows–
Etched there with their rocking feet.
Is fashioned too, by every beat
    Of shirt and sheet.

Still her clothing is less risky
Than her body in its prime,
They are chain–stitched and so is she
Chain–stitched to her soul for time.
Ravelling grandly into vice
Dropping crooked into rhyme.
Slipping through the stitch of virtue,
        Into crime.

Though her lips are vague as fancy
In her youth–
They bloom vivid and repulsive
As the truth.
Even vases in the making
        Are uncouth.

In Particular

WHAT loin-cloth, what rag of wrong
  Unpriced?
What turn of body, what of lust
Undiced?
So we've worshipped you a little
More than Christ.

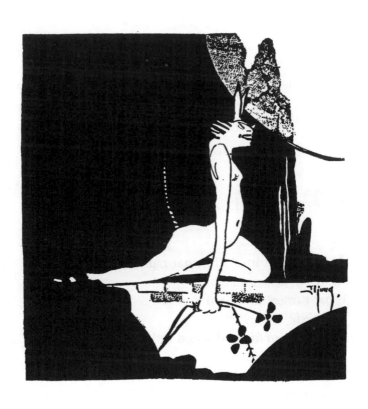

Twilight of the Illicit

YOU, with your long blank udders
        And your calms,
Your spotted linen and your
Slack'ning arms.
With satiated fingers dragging
At your palms.

Your knees set far apart like
Heavy spheres;
With discs upon your eyes like

Husks of tears;
And great ghastly loops of gold
Snared in your ears.

Your dying hair hand–beaten
'Round your head.
Lips, long lengthened by wise words
Unsaid.
And in your living all grimaces
Of the dead.

One sees you sitting in the sun
Asleep;
With the sweeter gifts you had
And didn't keep,
One grieves that the altars of
Your vice lie deep.

You, the twilight powder of
A fire–wet dawn;
You, the massive mother of
Illicit spawn;
While the others shrink in virtue
You have borne.

We'll see you staring in the sun
A few more years,
With discs upon your eyes like

Husks of tears;
And great ghastly loops of gold
Snared in your ears.

To a Cabaret Dancer

A THOUSAND lights had smitten her
  Into this thing;
Life had taken her and given her
  One place to sing.

She came with laughter wide and calm;
  And splendid grace;
And looked between the lights and wine
  For one fine face.

And found life only passion wide
  'Twixt mouth and wine.

She ceased to search, and growing wise
  Became less fine.

Yet some wondrous thing within the mess
  Was held in check:–
Was missing as she groped and clung
  About his neck.

One master chord we couldn't sound
  For lost the keys,
Yet she hinted of it as she sang
  Between our knees.

We watched her come with subtle fire
  And learned feet,
Stumbling among the lustful drunk
  Yet somehow sweet

We saw the crimson leave her cheeks
  Flame in her eyes;
For when a woman lives in awful haste
  A woman dies.

The jests that lit our hours by night
  And made them gay,
Soiled a sweet and ignorant soul
  And fouled its play.

Barriers and heart both broken—dust
   Beneath her feet.
You've passed her forty times and sneered
   Out in the street.

A thousand jibes had driven her
   To this at last;
Till the ruined crimson of her lips
   Grew vague and vast.

Until her songless soul admits
   Time comes to kill:
You pay her price and wonder why
   You need her still.

Suicide

Corpse A
> THEY brought her in, a shattered small
>   Cocoon,
> With a little bruisèd body like
> A startled moon;
> And all the subtle symphonies of her
> A twilight rune.

Corpse B

THEY gave her hurried shoves this way
        And that.
Her body shock–abbreviated
As a city cat.
She lay out listlessly like some small mug
Of beer gone flat.

DJUNA BARNES

Long seen as a legendary figure by her admirers, Djuna Barnes has increasingly come to be recognized over the past few decades as a major American author. She is best known for her fictional masterwork, *Nightwood,* an anatomy; but she also wrote other works of fiction, *A Book* (reprinted as *A Night Among the Horses* and later, with new stories and substantial revisions, as *Spillway*) and *Ryder.* She also published an almanac, *Ladies Almanack,* and a drama, *The Antiphon.* Sun & Moon Press has published a selection of her early stories as *Smoke and Other Early Stories,* selected her theatrical interviews in *Interviews,* and brought together several of her writings on New York City in *New York.* Other books planned are *Poe's Mother: Selected Drawings; At the Roots of the Stars: The Short Plays; Collected Stories; Biography of Julie von Bartmann; Ann Portuguise;* and a new edition of *The Antiphon.*

With Eugene O'Neill and Edna St. Vincent Millay, Barnes was an early member of the Provincetown Players. Later, in the 1920s, she lived in Paris, where her wit and brilliant writing won her close friendships with T.S. Eliot, James Joyce, Peggy Guggenheim, and other well-known American expatriates. When she returned to the United States, she wrote for *The Theater Guild Magazine.* She died in New York in 1982.

SUN & MOON CLASSICS

This publication was made possible, in part, through an operational grant from the Andrew W. Mellon Foundation and through contributions from the following individuals:

Charles Altieri (Seattle, Washington)
John Arden (Galway, Ireland)
Paul Auster (Brooklyn, New York)
Jesse Huntley Ausubel (New York, New York)
Dennis Barone (West Hartford, Connecticut)
Jonathan Baumbach (Brooklyn, New York)
Guy Bennett (Los Angeles, California)
Bill Berkson (Bolinas, California)
Steve Benson (Berkeley, California)
Charles Bernstein and Susan Bee (New York, New York)
Dorothy Bilik (Silver Spring, Maryland)
Alain Bosquet (Paris, France)
In Memoriam: John Cage
In Memoriam: Camilo José Cela
Bill Corbett (Boston, Massachusetts)
Fielding Dawson (New York, New York)
Robert Crosson (Los Angeles, California)
Tina Darragh and P. Inman (Greenbelt, Maryland)
Christopher Dewdney (Toronto, Canada)
Arkadii Dragomoschenko (St. Petersburg, Russia)
George Economou (Norman, Oklahoma)
Kenward Elmslie (Calais, Vermont)
Elaine Equi and Jerome Sala (New York, New York)
Lawrence Ferlinghetti (San Francisco, California)
Richard Foreman (New York, New York)
Howard N. Fox (Los Angeles, California)
Jerry Fox (Aventura, Florida)
In Memoriam: Rose Fox
Melvyn Freilicher (San Diego, California)
Miro Gavran (Zagreb, Croatia)
Allen Ginsberg (New York, New York)
Peter Glassgold (Brooklyn, New York)
Barbara Guest (New York, New York)
Perla and Amiram V. Karney (Bel Air, California)

Fred Haines (Los Angeles, California)
Václav Havel (Prague, The Czech Republic)
Lyn Hejinian (Berkeley, California)
Fanny Howe (La Jolla, California)
Harold Jaffe (San Diego, California)
Ira S. Jaffe (Albuquerque, New Mexico)
Pierre Joris (Albany, New York)
Alex Katz (New York, New York)
Tom LaFarge (New York, New York)
Mary Jane Lafferty (Los Angeles, California)
Michael Lally (Santa Monica, California)
Norman Lavers (Jonesboro, Arkansas)
Jerome Lawrence (Malibu, California)
Stacey Levine (Seattle, Washington)
Herbert Lust (Greenwich, Connecticut)
Norman MacAffee (New York, New York)
Rosemary Macchiavelli (Washington, DC)
Beatrice Manley (Los Angeles, California)
In Memoriam: Mary McCarthy
Harry Mulisch (Amsterdam, The Netherlands)
Iris Murdoch (Oxford, England)
Martin Nakell (Los Angeles, California)
In Memoriam: bpNichol
Toby Olson (Philadelphia, Pennsylvania)
Maggie O'Sullivan (Hebden Bridge, England)
Rochelle Owens (Norman, Oklahoma)
Marjorie and Joseph Perloff (Pacific Palisades, California)
Dennis Phillips (Los Angeles, California)
Carl Rakosi (San Francisco, California)
Tom Raworth (Cambridge, England)
David Reed (New York, New York)
Ishmael Reed (Oakland, California)
Janet Rodney (Santa Fe, New Mexico)
Joe Ross (Washington, DC)
Jerome and Diane Rothenberg (Encinitas, California)
Dr. Marvin and Ruth Sackner (Miami Beach, Florida)
Floyd Salas (Berkeley, California)
Tom Savage (New York, New York)
Leslie Scalapino (Oakland, California)
James Sherry (New York, New York)
Aaron Shurin (San Francisco, California)

SUN & MOON CLASSICS